ROBERT ELMER

AstroKids

7

The Super-Duper Blooper

BETHANY BACKYARD®
www.bethanyhouse.com

Published by Bethany House Publishers
A Ministry of Bethany Fellowship International
11400 Hampshire Avenue South
Bloomington, Minnesota 55438
www.bethanyhouse.com

Printed in the United States of America by
Bethany Press International, Bloomington, Minnesota 55438

Library of Congress Cataloging-in-Publication Data

Elmer, Robert
    The super-duper blooper / by Robert Elmer.
        p. cm. — (AstroKids ; 7)
Summary: DeeBee's chance to co-star with the famous Neta Neutron on her holo-vid show would mean betraying her friends and drone, MAC, and even changing her name. Includes facts about man-made satellites and instructions for decoding a secret message.
    ISBN 0-7642-2627-4 (pbk.)
    [1. Space stations—Fiction. 2. Christian life—Fiction. 3. Science fiction.] I. Title.
    PZ7.E4794 Su 2002
    [Fic]—dc21   2002001342

To my sister, Joanie,
who's always young at heart.

Books by Robert Elmer

AstroKids

Promise of Zion

Adventures Down Under

The Young Underground

Robert

Freckles

ROBERT ELMER is an Earth-based author who writes for life-forms all over the solar system. Not long ago, he, his son Stefan, and the family dog, Freckles, were in a TV commercial—for about three seconds. They walked in front of a house for sale. The commercial was not broadcast all over the solar system, but only on local cable, about ninety-three million miles from the sun. Oh well!

Contents

✳ ✳ ✳

MEET THE
AstroKids

Lamar "Buzz" Bright

Show the way, Buzz! The
leader of the AstroKids
always has a great plan. He
also loves Jupiter ice cream.

Daphne "DeeBee" Ortiz

DeeBee's the brains of the
bunch—she can build or fix
almost anything. But, suffering satellites, don't tell her
she's a "GEEN-ius"!

Theodore "Tag" Ortiz

Yeah, DeeBee's little brother, Tag, always tags along. Count on him to say something silly at just the wrong time. He's in orbit.

Kumiko "Miko" Sało

Everybody likes Miko the stowaway. They just don't know how she got to be a karate master, or how she knows so much about space shuttles.

Vladimir "Mir" Chekhov

So his dad's the station commander and Mir usually gets his way? Give him a break! He's trying. And whatever he did, it was probably just a joke.

Live! From
1 CLEO-7!

* * *

"LIGHTS!"

Did I sound like a holo-vid director just then? I must have. My little brother, Tag, was staring up at me like I was some kind of alien.

"In three, everyone." I lowered my voice. Maybe that would help. "Places."

But Tag still looked surprised.

"Are you sure you're feeling all right, DeeBee? This isn't like you."

Maybe not like the *old* DeeBee Ortiz, first-class techno-nerd. This was the new me: DeeBee Ortiz, holo-vid superstar!

"QUIET ON THE SET!" I shouted. That's what holo-vid superstars are supposed to say, right? Three, two, one . . .

"And now, live from *CLEO*-7." I used my very best, very smooth announcer voice. "Three hundred eighty-four thousand, six hundred twenty-nine point zero three kilometers from Earth, in geosynchronous orbit—"

"Cut!" Tag waved his hands back and forth. "You're slipping into tech talk, DeeBee. Nobody knows what geo-sink is."

"Geo-SINK-run-us," I corrected him.

"Whatever. We don't get it."

"We?"

QUESTION 01:

Hate to say it so soon, but Tag's right. Most of us can hardly *pronounce* that word. What does it mean?

ANSWER 01:

Geosynchronous means something is parked in orbit above the Earth ... like a satellite or a space station. Picture yourself running around a merry-go-round, keeping up with your friend riding a merry-go-round horse. That's what a geosynchronous orbit looks like.

"Hey!" My brother hopped up and down.

"What happened to the big show, DeeBee?"

Right. I cleared my throat. I could do this. "We're up here on *CLEO*-7 to give you . . ."

(You can clap now. Go ahead. Let's hear it.)

"The DeeBee Ortiz and the AstroKids Show!"

"Whooo! Yeah!" When Tag started whooping, all the other AstroKids joined in: Buzz, Miko, and Mir, who grinned his VBG. (That stands for Very Big Grin.)

They liked me! Who says DeeBee Ortiz is just a boring space nerd? An orbit head? A brainiac?

Not the AstroKids. And not my drone, MAC, either.

MAC was floating all around us, turning up lights, waving his arms like crazy, and pretty much just having a droney kind of good time. He's homemade but still a top-notch drone. Zero-G was having fun, too, snuffling around the floor like all dogs do and making funny comments like most dogs don't. (You know about his M2V collar, don't you? That stands for Mind 2 Voice. It lets Zero-G talk like a person.)

As for me, I was just getting warmed up.

"Today, folks, we have a great program, FYI."

Meaning, For Your Information.

"With a great guest."

I waved my hand at Mir.

"And of course I'm going to show you a few of my latest inventions. But first, let's meet Dr. Mir Chekhov, who has just made an incredible discovery in . . ."

Let's see. What could Dr. Chekhov be an expert in?

"Hyper-ion drive physics?" guessed Mir. Not bad. He was doing okay so far, playing the part of the special guest.

"That's right!" I stabbed the air over my head. "Now, for fifty million, can you tell the audience what comets are made of?"

"Uh, well . . ." Mir looked to the others for help. No go.

"Okay, for thirty million." I would give him an easier question, just to be nice. "Who invented micro-warp physics?"

Another blank stare. "What's that?"

I sighed. Maybe this interview was going to be harder than I thought.

"Okay, Doctor. For ten million, then. Who's

the commander of *CLEO-7*?"

Mir's face brightened. "My dad!"

"Yes! You win ten million. Congratulations."

Mir bowed and waved to the pretend crowd while everyone clapped again. Remind me not to enter Mir into any real-life trivia contests, though. I mean, the poor guy tries, but . . . well, you know what I mean. Of course, I wasn't going to make him feel bad about not knowing basic scientific facts. Techno-nerds like me need all the friends we can get.

And anyway, we were just playing around. Like, HHOK. **Ha Ha, Only Kidding.** I was only pretending to be a famous holo-vid host, with pretend famous guests.

But, famous-shmaymus, things sure got out of hand in a hurry. That silly, pretend holo-vid show started this whole major mess. And if I knew then what I know now . . .

Believe me, I would have been happy staying a nobody techno-nerd. In fact, I probably would have locked the door to my shop and never come out.

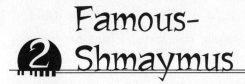 Famous-Shmaymus

Out of hand.

Out of control.

Crazy.

Don't believe me? Just check out hallway 765-E, four days later. (That would be AstroDate 09-25-2175.)

"Hey, congratulations, DeeBee!" A tekkie in a bright blue jumpsuit came up and gave me a big hug.

I almost couldn't breathe.

Thing is, I hardly knew her. Sure, she worked with my dad in the data lab. But now, all of a sudden, she acted as if we were VBGFL. Very Best Girl Friends for Life.

What was up?

"You'll be sure to tell Neta Neutron we're good friends, won't you?"

"Uh . . ."

"See, I have this nice little song I've been working on, and I know she would just *love* it if she heard it."

The tekkie started to belt out a powerfully sorry version of "Ya Saturn My Achin' Breakin' Heart Till It Done Broke in Two."

"And there ain't no way in the galax-ahye . . ." She planted a hand on her heart.

Oh dear. I had to get away from her.

Fast.

Either that, or my ears would be scarred for life.

"I will wear your *RIIIINGS*," she screeched.

Zero-G howled, and I did my best not to scream in pain.

"I, uh, have to get going," I told her. "Thanks for sharing."

Even MAC couldn't take it. His overload lights were blinking. Poor drone. He doesn't handle those kinds of noises very well.

"Oh, my aching circuits," he said.

The tekkie didn't seem to notice. "So what do

you think?" she asked. The smile never left her lips.

"Well, that's a lovely song, I'm sure." I tried to be polite.

Only, the way she sang it wasn't so lovely. I walked faster down the hallway. Get me outta here!

But you know the old Earth expression: It's like going from a nova to a supernova. By the time I reached my lab, another bunch of people was already there to mob me. Yes, me, space nerd DeeBee.

Nothing wrong with being all of a sudden popular. But they all wanted me to talk to Neta Neutron for them, too. Like I had an "in" with the most famous holo-vid star in the solar system!

I tried to tell them I'd never met Neta Neutron. In fact, I had only talked to her once on a far-space interface. Naturally, she was between shows on her Moon Colony 12 set.

Want to know what she said? Imagine this really thick lunar accent.

"You're just poifect for the show, dahling. Beeyooteefool. I just a-DORE the way you talk to the camera. That face. That voice. You're a natural."

Right. A natural nerd. (I didn't say that. Just thought it.) She had caught me at a bad time.

"You really want to talk to *me*?" I had said. "You want to talk to *me* about being on your show?"

"Of course, dahling. I need a new co-star. Someone with a science background. An inventor might be poifect."

"But how did you. . . ? And why are you. . . ?"

I sure didn't sound too smart just then. But how often do *you* talk to the most famous vid star in the solar system?

"Never you mind, precious. We'll chat next week when I come to your cozy little station. I'm going to put you on my show for a week. We'll see if you work out. In the meantime, you just get ready to be famous."

Suffering satellites! A week with Neta Neutron!

"But what about my friends?" The other AstroKids would have been proud of me for saying this. They would have liked that I didn't forget them. "Can they—"

"Oh, you mean the other ones on the holo-vid? Of course, bring them along if it makes you feel better. Toodle-oo, dahling."

Right. Toodle-oo.

Before I could ask her anything else, Neta hung up, just like that. Gone.

I guess vid stars do that sort of thing. But this was too weird. So, ladies and gentlemen, space travelers, astronauts, cosmonauts, argonauts, and kilowatts, here's . . .

The "Something Weird Is Going On at CLEO-7" Countdown:

Weird 04: Somehow Neta Neutron had a vid of me and my friends.

Weird 03: But I didn't send her the vid.

Weird 02: So where had the vid come from?

Weird 01: And who sent it to her?

I didn't know the answers—forget about Tag always saying I'm a GEEN-ius.

I was confused.

I was confounded.

I was mixed up, muddled, and befuddled.

And for once, I didn't have the foggiest what was going on. I mean, what was the deal with being a natural and making me famous and all that?

Right.

Famous-shmaymus.

YG2BK. As in, You've Got 2 Be Kidding.

But I found out a week later that Neta Neutron wasn't kidding about coming to *CLEO-7*.

Not at all. And that's when my troubles really began.

3 Simply Smashing ✳ ✳ ✳

"No, no, no, no, no!" Neta Neutron yelled at one of her helpers. (That's five times. I counted.) "Percee, I want this stage over here by these trees. Here! Didn't you hear me?"

Well, I think he did. Everybody on the station must have heard, too, from the tekkies in the labs to shuttle workers in the hub and people all the way around to the dining hall. This beautiful woman rushed around the *CLEO-7* space garden telling her people what to do. She was pretty good at bossing Percee Plasma around, too.

QUESTION 02:
   A garden? On a space station?
ANSWER 02:
   Yep, and it's my favorite place, with little trees and bushes and other growing things. Even a fountain.

So anyway, this Percee fellow grunted and groaned and pushed the platform over to where she wanted it, just the way she told him.

I'd shaken his hand just a few minutes before. Ever grabbed a dead fish by the tail?

Ah, so you know what I mean.

"Percee!" wailed Miss Neutron. "More lights on my hair, dahling. It's dreadfully dreary in here."

"Does she call everybody darling?" asked Tag. I was wondering the same thing. "Because if she calls *me* that, I'm going to tell her my name is Theodore."

"She can call *me* darling." Mir pushed his way past Buzz to the front of our fan club line. He tried to get Neta Neutron to look our way.

Talk about a silly thing to say. But I admit Neta Neutron looked like a vid star, all right. Maybe it was her beautiful blond hair, or the bright green eyes, or the perfect Milky Way skin.

"Shhh." I pushed the button on my e-reader pad to check my tryout lines. How could I remember all this? The words swam across the screen: "Hi, my name is Daphne Orr." (That was a typo, of course. My last name is Ortiz, not Orr. And nobody calls me Daphne, except Mom and Dad.) "And I want to show you some of my inventions from here on *CLEO-7*."

"What about us?" Buzz wanted to know. "When do you talk about the rest of us?"

MAC was circling the group, satellite-style. Zero-G was orbiting, too, but on the floor. Miko politely waited her turn. (She was a girl, after all!) But the boys were being kind of obnoxious.

You know, a pain.

"I don't know when I talk about you." I shrugged. "I don't see anything on my e-reader about you guys yet."

"But that's the whole point!" Mir threw up his hands. "That's why I sent her our vi—" He bit his tongue.

Wait a minute. What?

"It was *you*!" I grabbed Mir's shoulders so he wouldn't get away. "You're the one who sent Neta Neutron our vid."

Mir tried to look cool. But there was no escape. He even wore a little grin.

"What vid are you talking about?" he asked. "I didn't do it."

"You know exactly what I'm talking about."

But Mir just put out his hands, the way he does when somebody catches him at one of his practical jokes. Like switching all the station computer voices to Chinese, or making all the station drones go wacko. Maybe you remember that one.

"I'll never tell," he said, like it was all a joke. "You can tickle me until I bust. But I'll never squeal."

"Aaaa-huum." Did you know drones can clear their throats? Mine can. "I must confess something, Mistress DeeBee."

"Oh, so now it's Mir and MAC, partners in crime?" Buzz adjusted his Hollywood-style sunshades. "This show is getting better and better."

"I recorded you pretending last week," the drone told us. So what else was new? Everything MAC saw and heard stayed in his memory files. That's how he works.

"But Mir pulled my files," MAC said. "And he did not ask."

Now I got it. Mir had taken MAC's mem files

and zipped them off to Neta Neutron.

"Hey, I thought you'd be really jazzed." Mir was still trying to wiggle out of this.

"Aren't you happy, DeeBee?" Tag turned to me, too. "We're all going to be super-duper famous now. You heard what Neta Neutron told you."

What could I say? Everybody else was so excited. Maybe Mir's plan was okay this time. NHD. No Harm Done.

"Oh, this is simply smashing!" Zero-G jumped up on his back legs and twirled around. "We can discuss my favorite cat chases, or the station's ten best sniffs. Dogs all over the solar system will finally have a show of their own!"

Finally, I let Mir's shoulders go. I couldn't stay upset at him—especially when he cracked his crazy grin.

"Well . . ." I said.

Anyway, mystery solved. We all gathered around for a big galactic salute. Everybody in a circle, their right hand up, little pinkie out. One, two, three . . .

"Goooooooooo, AstroKids!" we all yelled. I

had to smile, too. We were in this together. Maybe this was going to be okay, after all.

"Next up!" Percee Plasma checked his e-reader. "Daphne Orr and the Asteroid Kids."

Beware the
4 Gaffer Drones

$* * *$

"That's ASTRO kids." Tag would, of course, be the one to correct Percee Plasma. "Not asteroid. And her name is—"

"Shh," I told him. "Don't be rude."

Right then, the lights came up bright as a supernova at noon. And when I took one teeny step forward, Miss Neta Neutron put her hands on her hips and looked at us as if we were crashing her party.

"Gaffers!" she cried. "Grips! Over here!"

Gaffers? Grips? Yeowch! That sounded mean. What had we done now?

Like I said, Neta Neutron sure knew how to boss people around. She told her fancy mirror-drones where to go, too. They were like our station drones, but polished so brightly you could hardly look at them without shades. These drones swarmed all over the place, setting up lights above our heads or floating sound gizmos next to the stage.

Bzzzzeeep! They all buzzed around double-time when she clapped her hands or snapped her fingers.

"Wow," whispered Tag. "*Looc.*" (That's Tag-talk for *cool.*)

QUESTION 03:

Uh, excuse me, but is it too late to ask what gaffers and grips are? Are they spacey show biz put downs?

ANSWER 03:

That's what I thought at first. But I found out gaffers are the chief electro-experts. And grips help move scenery and backgrounds. Next time you see a vid, check out the credits at the end for gaffers and grips.

"Daphne dahling!" Neta Neutron looked right at me with her great green eyes. And when she pointed at me, her blue fingernails sparkled. "I'm so glad to see you. Come, come, come."

"You mean me?" I looked around just to be sure.

"Yes, yes, yes. Your name *is* Daphne, is it not?"

"Right." I gulped. So this was my big chance. The old DeeBee was behind me. The new *Daphne*, ahead. "That's me."

"But only Mom and Dad call her Daphne," added Tag. "She doesn't like it."

Neta Neutron squinted at the rest of the AstroKids as if she was seeing them for the first time.

"And *whooo* are *theeey*?"

"They're my friends." I answered. "Remember you said they could come?"

(Long pause.) "Oh, did I?"

"Yeah, 'cause we're part of the show!" piped up Tag. "We're the other kids from the holo-vid, remember?"

"Of course." She sounded like she'd just found a three-inch Martian glowworm floating in her milk. She whispered something to Percee, who nodded.

"And I'm the one who sent you the vid." Mir put his hands on his hips and planted his gripper shoes on the deck. "We're *all* going to try out for your show. Isn't that right, DeeBee?"

Neta Neutron acted as if she didn't hear. She snapped her long fingers.

"Percee dahling, have one of our drones bring these guests a plate of soda disks and Astro-Cheesies, will you?"

"AstroCheesies?" Mir and Buzz gave each other the thumbs-up.

Boys and food, right?

But Miss Neutron wasn't quite finished.

"And please have the gaffer drones remove that horrid trash bucket over there. Right away."

Trash bucket? All I could see was my good old drone, MAC. He must have followed us to see what was going on.

"Pardon me," he droned. "You must be mistaken. I am not a trash bucket, though I have been put together with two kilograms of used and recycled materials. I am your Micro-Automated

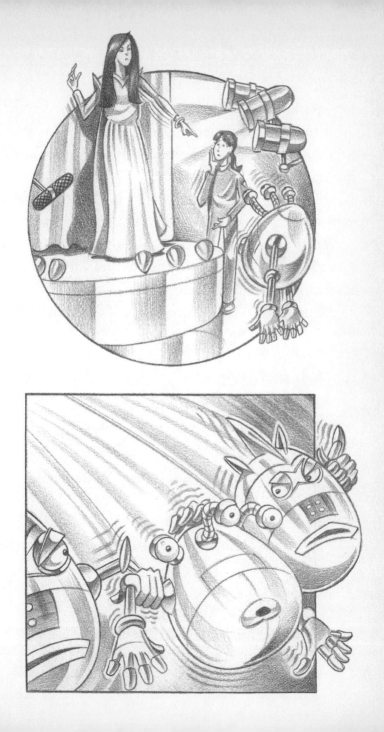

Companion, and I am here to—"

"Aaagh!" screamed Neta Neutron. "Get that, that . . . *thing* out of here before he gives one of my drones a computer virus."

"Oh no, I am quite healthy. Not even the sniffles. Mistress DeeBee—"

But he didn't have time to finish. A couple of Neta Neutron's mirror-drones flew up to him and started to carry him away.

"But wait!" MAC squawked. "You cannot do this!"

The Adventures of DeeBee's Conscience, Episode 1

Neta Neutron: "Gracious!" (She fans her cheek.) "Do you have any idea where such a dreadful piece of junk could have come from?"

DeeBee: "Well . . ."

Tag: "He belongs to—"

(DeeBee clamps her hand over her little brother's mouth.)

Tag: "My ffifffterr!"

Neta Neutron: "Pardon?"

DeeBee's Conscience: *Warning, warning!*

Stretching the
5 Truth

✳ ✳ ✳

"My brother's always saying funny things," I told Neta Neutron right after she had MAC hauled out of the room.

It *was* true.

No way was I going to tell her that "horrid trash bucket" was mine. What would she think of me then? Once a techno-nerd, always a techno-nerd? Now that I was here, no way was I going to sink this tryout.

"Tag just meant . . ." I tried again. Should I tell her the whole truth?

No. Better not to claim my homemade drone for now. After all, MAC *was* just a drone. Drones don't have feelings.

Do they?

Tag wiggled out of my grip and scowled at me like I'd punched him in the stomach.

"I think I'll go check on MAC," he said. And then he huffed away.

Well, I didn't have time to worry about it. Just then, two of Miss Neutron's cool mirror-drones came at me with face powder and stage makeup.

Hey, this was more like it. Very un-nerdy. Except that my nose started to twitch . . .

Ker-CHOOO!

"It'll be okay, DeeBee," Miko stepped over and told me. "There's no hurry. We'll watch. We'll get our turn to be on the show later."

Good old Miko. She was always saying nice things like that.

"Thanks," I told her. "I'm sure you're right."

"All right, now." Miss Neutron clapped her hands again. "I'm glad that's over. We're ready for Miss Daphne Orr."

What?

"Er, Miss Neutron?" I didn't want to sound rude, but . . . "It's Ortiz."

Neta Neutron leaned close, like she had a secret for me.

"Orr just sounds more . . . *professional*, don't you think? A poifect stage name." She lowered her voice and looked around. "Nothing against Ortiz, of course."

Right. My family had always been proud of how my grandfather Alejandro Ortiz had been the first deep-space pilot from Puerto Rico. Ortiz was a good name, and I *liked* it. But maybe keeping it for the show didn't matter so much, after all.

"Any questions?" she asked with a fresh, new vid-star smile.

I swallowed hard. "Actually, I was wondering about my friends. When do they get a chance to be on your show?"

"Ah yes. I've been meaning to tell you about that." She fluttered her long lashes and gave me a longer look.

"You're wonderful on camera, Daphne. Just what I'm looking for. But right now, I'm really not interested in doing a program with all your asteroid friends."

That would be *AstroKids*. But I couldn't say anything. Not about changing my name, not about leaving out my friends. It was like my tongue was stuck inside my mouth.

"I'm sure you understand, dear. It's nothing personal."

"But . . ." I couldn't believe it. "But we're . . . a team. We were supposed to do this together."

"Oh, how sweet. I like that."

"So—"

"Let me put it plainly, dahling: You can choose between being on the show or playing with your asteroid gang. One or the other. Not both. You do understand, don't you, Daphne?"

"Actually." I scraped my foot on the floor. "Everybody calls me DeeBee."

Neta Neutron laughed.

"Spunky. That's what I like about you, Daphne dahling. So, it's all settled."

I cleared my throat and looked over at my friends. They were standing at the edge of the space garden. Miko smiled. Buzz waved. Mir gave me the thumbs-up sign. But that was only because they couldn't hear a word Neta Neutron was saying.

Good thing.

The Adventures of DeeBee's Conscience, Episode 2

DeeBee's Conscience: *This is where you speak up, DeeBee.*

DeeBee: "Uh . . ."

DeeBee's Conscience: *Come on, say something!*

DeeBee: "Well . . ."

"Splendid," said Neta Neutron. "I knew you'd understand. Let's get the rest of this makeup on and continue our tryout, shall we?"

Splendid-shmlendid. I felt sick while we got ready to film the new *Neta Neutron Show*. Co-hosted by (clap here if you want to) . . . "the amazing Daph-neeeeee Orr!"

I had to admit Percee did a pretty good job as announcer. His voice was deep enough to rattle your chest from a couple of light-years away. And you should have seen the snazzy special effects they were going to use.

FLASH! (That was a strobe light.)

ZWAAP! (A laser.)

POOOF! (And that was me, jumping out of a cloud of smoke.)

It looked pretty good. But inside, I still felt terrible. Have you ever sneaked a cookie your mom told you not to eat? I did once, when I was four. I still remember the feeling. At first, the cookie tasted good. Then it sat like a gritty asteroid in my tummy.

That's how it felt to practice my first show with the famous Neta Neutron.

Still, maybe I was going to be famous, too, all over the solar system. DeeBee—I mean, Daphne Orr, Famous Inventor. That part sounded okay, mostly because no one would ever think I was just an astro-nerd again.

Yep, this was a new me, all right. Everybody in the station was clapping and cheering. I should have felt great.

But all I felt was sick.

Sick, when I thought of all the ways I'd already sold out.

The "Daphne Orr Sells Out" Countdown

Sellout 03: I never told Neta Neutron MAC was my drone.

Sellout 02: I let her change my perfectly good name for the show. And why had she done it? Did she think it sounded too Puerto Rican?

Sellout 01: Worst of all, my friends still thought they were going to be on the show, too! And I was too chicken to tell them differently.

Ever hear of a space chicken? Me, I felt like I had feathers all over. But I also knew one thing: I would not, could not go back to being an astro-nerd. No way, José. Not in a million light-years. So I wouldn't let this chance pass me by. After rehearsal, I would go straight to my shop and get my inventions ready for the first show.

And after I told them the bad news, I would patch things up somehow with Mir and Buzz and Miko . . . even Tag.

Only how?

Daphne vs.

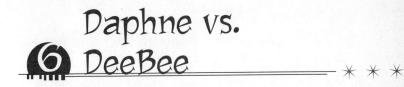

6 DeeBee

✳ ✳ ✳

Remember my job from the last chapter? Patch things up with the other AstroKids.

That's all I could think about during my first rehearsal. I thought about it while Neta Neutron showed me how the lights worked. I thought about it when I read my practice lines from the floating screen. And I thought about it when I learned how to smile into the camera.

Sure, I worried about getting my inventions ready for the real show. But more than that, I wanted to make sure the other AstroKids would still like me.

The Adventures of DeeBee's Conscience, Episode 3

DeeBee's Conscience: *So, when are you going to tell your friends?*

DeeBee: "You mean about them not being on the *Neta Neutron Show?*"

DeeBee's Conscience: *Exactly. Your brother's been telling everybody on the station he's going to be on the show with you. Some of the younger kids are even asking him for his autograph.*

DeeBee: "I know, I know. I just don't know how to tell them the truth without hurting their feelings."

A second later, I nearly blasted off at the sound of Miko's voice behind me.

"There you are, DeeBee. I should have known you'd be here."

(My heartbeat: Two hundred plus. *Ba-BOOM, ba-BOOM . . .*)

"Oh." You know how it is when somebody catches you talking to yourself? "I wasn't talking to anybody. I was just, uh . . ."

"That's okay." Miko didn't make a big deal out of it. "I talk to myself all the time. But what's the story about hurting someone's feelings? Something I should know about?"

That's when the boys came rumbling into the

space garden. And you know how boys are. They're always making lots of noise, pushing each other, that sort of thing. We could hear them light-years away.

"Hey, DeeBee." Mir could clown with the best of them. "What's up with the rich and famous?"

"We were just talking." Miko gave them a "we girls stick together and you don't know what you're talking about" look.

Mir pointed his nose at the ceiling. "Ooooh, and we can't? I guess the star can't talk to us common folks, huh?"

"Wait a minute. You're getting ahead of yourselves." I decided it was now or never. "I have to tell you guys something. You, too, Miko."

"A message from Her Majesty, Queen Dee-Beedala!" Mir really was taking this too far. "Maybe Her Highness is finally going to tell us when we're going to be on the show."

Okay. Deep breath.

"You're not."

For a short minute, all you could hear was the station's soft hum. A few clicks and whirrs, the usual stuff.

Then Buzz started to chuckle. "Hee-hee. That's pretty good. You really had us there, for a micro-second."

My little brother caught the giggles, too. "Yeah, DeeBee. (Ha-ha.) That's pretty (ha-ha) funny. We're not going to be on the show. Sure!"

Pretty soon, everybody was laughing.

Everybody except me. Because then I had to repeat what Neta Neutron had told me. And as I kept talking, their laughs got softer and softer.

Miko was the first one to really catch on. "We're, ah, happy for you, DeeBee." She gulped and jabbed Mir in the ribs. "Aren't we, boys?"

Tag snapped his mouth shut. (It was hanging open.) But he didn't answer her.

"What was I supposed to tell Miss Neutron?" I asked.

Mir shrugged. No more VBGs from him. "How about 'gooooooo, AstroKids?' " he asked.

He *would* have to remind me of that.

The Adventures of DeeBee's Conscience, Episode 4

DeeBee: "Don't they get it? It's not my fault! I mean, suffering satellites. Can I help it if Miss

Neutron wants only *me* on the show?"

DeeBee's Conscience: *It's your decision, but if you ask me . . .*

DeeBee: "What was I supposed to do? Tell her no?"

Well, I knew one thing for sure. I had lots of questions, but not so many answers. A minute later, I was the only one left in the space garden. Buzz said they had to go.

That gave me plenty of time to think. And, sure, ICBW. **I Could Be Wrong.** But I decided if this was how a space nerd was supposed to make lots of friends, something wasn't working.

And if it wasn't working, I would just have to fix it.

Right. That was easy for *Daphne* to say.

DeeBee wasn't so sure.

Lights! Action!
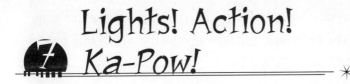 ## Ka-Pow! ✳ ✳ ✳

"Lights!"

The next morning, I kept my eye on one of Neta Neutron's floating mirror-drones, the one with a fold-out bright yellow screen. All I had to do was read the words on the screen.

I looked down at the floor for my box of inventions. The pocket float chair and the booster boots were ready. And so was my latest, the 3-second style helmet.

But they were gone!

"Miss Neutron!" I whispered. "My—"

"Not to worry, dahling." She held up her hand and smiled. "Percee's taken care of all that for you. Just read your lines."

Just then Percee Plasma slipped in with another armload of stuff. Not mine, by the way.

"I'm sorry, dear," said Miss Neutron, "but we

took the liberty of giving you new props. I'm sure you won't mind. These are much nicer looking than those rusty old things you had. Don't you think?"

Rusty?

"But, but . . ."

"In five, everyone!" Percee left the new inventions at my feet and took his place off set.

"Four, three . . ."

This wasn't play or rehearsal anymore. This was the real thing. The big time. The *Neta Neutron Show*, live from *CLEO-7*. With Neta's special guest, inventing genius Daphne Orr!

That's when people started clapping—my folks, even the rest of the AstroKids. Everybody was standing around, watching. Come to think of it, the whole *solar system* was watching. What could I do now?

So after Neta Neutron started things off, the green light on my reader started blinking and I began reading.

"HI, I'M DAPHNE ORR, AND I INVENT THINGS." (REACH DOWN.) "THINGS LIKE THIS NEAT INSTO-TRANSLATOR."

Okay, so it looked a lot slicker than my own insto-translator. But the idea was to wear the earphones and hear your own language, no matter what the other person was speaking. Only this slick-looking version didn't work that well.

"AND THIS IS A BUMP-AWAY PERSONAL FORCE-FIELD BELT I MADE FROM SPARE PARTS HERE IN THE *CLEO-7* WORKSHOP. LET ME EXPLAIN . . ."

Yeah, right. This belt looked like a fashion doodad and didn't have half the power mine did. But guess which one I had to hold up on the show?

"Oh, this is so mahvelous, dahling." Neta clapped her hands together as if she was seeing the gizmos for the first time. "Isn't it, everyone?"

The drone-cam turned just in time to catch the crowd holding up a bunch of big signs. You know, like they do for the *Good Morning, Moon* show?

I think my mom was holding one of them. Oh no.

We ♥ *Daphne.*

Or how about, *DeeBee Ortiz,* CLEO-7 *Is Proud of U!*

I kept going. And after the third commercial, I heard a funny noise from behind my chair, just as I was pulling out the last invention for the day.

"Do you have any more inventions for us, Daphne?" asked Neta.

She knew I did. I checked my reader screen to make sure.

"YES, I SURE DO. THIS IS MY SCIENCE FAIR DRONE PROJECT."

Only thing was, the drone I was going to show looked ten times glitzier than MAC, and it wasn't made with hand-me-down parts. I reached for it, but there was that noise again.

"Aaaa-huum."

I froze. And out of the corner of my eye, I saw what I was afraid of seeing.

"Pardon me, but I am your Micro-Automated Companion, and I—"

Oh dear. I don't know if anyone else could hear him, but MAC had somehow snuck in behind our chairs and was coming up right behind me.

I reached back and tried to stuff my clunky drone back behind my chair. Maybe no one would see him.

But he just popped back up. "It is now my turn!" he whispered.

"Ah-HEMM." I coughed loudly to cover his voice. And I never stopped smiling at the drone-cam.

Neta was good. Very good. Before I knew it, she had the cams all turn to her, so nobody watching would see the weird hide-and-seek game going on with MAC.

In a micro-second, Percee was on him like a Martian alley cat. He grabbed MAC from behind.

"This hunk of junk again?"

The Adventures of DeeBee's Conscience, Episode 5

DeeBee's Conscience: *DeeBee, please! You have to explain!*
DeeBee: "Hush! Not now!"

"I have no idea what this thing is." The words

slipped out of my mouth as Percee wrestled MAC away from the set. I thought MAC would put up a fight, but he just looked at me with his three sad eyes and let himself be carried away.

"Mistress DeeBee?" he squeaked.

I looked away and tried to keep from crying. I really did not want to cry in front of the whole solar system.

Oh, MAC. Why did you do this?

We finished that first show in a hurry. I showed off the perfect, pretty silver drone and read my lines, and everybody clapped when the Applause sign came on. They even laughed at some of my jokes. Still, I ran off the set as soon as the lights went out.

"Daphne dahling!" cried Neta. "You were mahvelous!"

Just then, though, I didn't feel too mahvelous. Mad, upset, and lots of things in between. But not mahvelous. Even less mahvelous when I reached my shop and saw MAC spinning in circles. Every time he spun, he crunched himself against the wall.

"What are you doing?" I tried to hold on to

him the way Percee had. But I wasn't strong enough.

He slipped away from me.

"I am going offline for a while. I need a drone vacation."

BASH! He made another hit to the shop wall, just above the garbage chute door.

"MAC, don't! You'll hurt your gyros!"

SMASH!

"What do you care?" he asked. "You do not know me. You said so yourself."

"MAC, look . . . everybody was watching. What was I supposed to say? You surprised me, that's all."

CRASH! I couldn't hold him back. Even homemade drones are stronger than they look. But how long could he keep crunching into the wall like that?

"Perhaps you should just *BASH!* replace me with one of those fancy mirror-drones," he told me.

"Stop it. There's no other drone like you."

I tried to slip in between MAC and the wall, but that didn't work, either. Instead, he grabbed the garbage chute door.

"MAC, watch out!"

"Good-bye, Daphne Orr."

WHOOOOOOOOOOSH!

Nothing But a
8 Hound Dog

✳ ✳ ✳

MAC was halfway into the garbage chute before I grabbed one of his arms. I could feel the duct tape around his elbow starting to loosen.

Riiiiip!

This might sound funny, but it wasn't. I'm sure MAC didn't know it, and maybe you don't, either, but the garbage chute goes straight to a crusher, then to a garbage shuttle aimed straight at the sun.

And when the garbage gets too close to the sun, well, *ffft!*

It's toast.

Suffering satellites! *Now* does it sound serious?

I hooked my toes around the door and held on, but MAC's arm was hanging by a laser thread.

"You have to help me!" I yelled at the top of

my lungs. I don't know if he heard, though. The *WHOOOOSH*ing sound was pretty loud. "I'm going to fall in with you if you don't!"

That's when I felt hands grab my ankles—real hands. By that time, I must have looked like a piece of Venusian taffy, all stretched out. I could just see myself going *kerrrrrr-SNAP!*

That's just about what happened. *Taa-WAAAANG!* A micro-second later, we all tumbled into a heap on the shop floor: MAC, me, and . . .

Mir.

"What's going on?" he asked. His wavy brown hair was standing on end. Mine probably looked even funnier. "Is that how you treat a friend?"

I know it looked bad, like I was trying to toss MAC into the trash. I would have asked the same thing, if I were Mir. I tried to catch my breath, tell Mir thank you, and explain. I didn't let go of MAC for a second. Not even when Percee Plasma and Neta Neutron burst into the room.

"That . . . that *thing* again!" Neta shrieked when she saw MAC. "It nearly ruined my show. Disable it, Percee. Destroy it. Demolish it—"

"No." I put my hand up to stop Percee. "I'll take care of it myself."

And before Mir could tell me no, I reached around and hit the Off switch under MAC's dented power panel. His arms went limp, and his lights went out.

The Adventures of DeeBee's Conscience, Episode 6

DeeBee's Conscience: *Uh-oh.*
DeeBee: (Blank look. No words.)

"Very good, dear." Neta Neutron fixed her already-perfect hair. "What a dreadful machine."

Mir got up, dusted himself off, and left. But his words kept echoing in my mind.

"Is that how you treat a friend?"

✳ ✳ ✳

Mir's words wouldn't go away, even hours later. So I tried repeating my own words.

"He's just a drone," I told myself. "He's just a drone."

Too bad I didn't believe myself. MAC was built from special parts my great-grandfather left me. And MAC may have looked frumpy, but he was very cool, almost like one of the AstroKids. Anybody would tell you that.

No, MAC *wasn't* just a drone.

But I couldn't tell the other kids I had taken him offline. I hoped Mir wouldn't say anything, either.

✳ ✳ ✳

That night, I tried to forget about MAC by working late, after everybody else had gone to bed.

EEE-yaw. That was a yawn.

I shook my head to stay awake. Maybe if I spiffed up my pocket float chair, Neta Neutron would let me talk about it on the show after all. I kept working.

EEEE-yaaawww. Yawns are catchy. You're probably thinking about yawning now, too. You can't help it.

And the booster boots worked great, except the duct tape made them look homemade. Maybe some shiny silver paint would fix that, or . . .

EEEEEE-yaaaaawwwww.

Before I knew it, I was face down on the workbench, catching up on Zs. Did an hour go by? Two? My face smooshed into a circuit board. I would have stayed asleep like that until morning, except I felt something slobbery on my hand.

Gross.

"Huh?" My eyes were kind of gummed shut. I yanked my hand up and wiped the drool from my cheek.

"Hey, there, Mistress DeeBee. Wake up."

Oh. It was only Zero-G. But what time was it? I looked up at the wall.

"Is it really 0200?" I groaned. "Two in the morning?"

"Correct." Don't ask me how Zero-G could be so perky when everybody else was supposed to be asleep. "I wanted to ask you something."

"Yeah?" I still wasn't quite awake.

"You see, I've been thinking that your show could use a co-host of the canine persuasion."

"A dog."

"I believe I said that. You need a dog on your show. A smart one, too. People love dogs. And I thought you might like to tell people about my collar, since it shows how smart I am. Cats aren't so smart, you know. In fact, if you gave one of them a collar . . ."

He went on like that. But remember what time it was? I rested my head again. And I started to think . . .

The "Three Ways Zero-G Can Be Annoying" Countdown

Annoying 03: Zero-G sometimes talks about rude things like drool and coughing up furballs and other gross things cats do.

Annoying 02: After that, he goes on and on about sniffing cat armpits and scarfing down nasty things like dust bunnies or old space suit lint.

Annoying 01: Sometimes he doesn't know when to stop. (Repeat Annoying 03 and Annoying 02.) Yuk. I think you get the idea.

"Are you listening, Mistress DeeBee?" Zero-G

again—of course. "Because if you're not, maybe you'd like to wake up with a game of chase. I could run, you could chase. What do you think?"

"I think I have a show to do tomorrow morning. And I think I need to get back to sleep. You too."

But Zero-G would not give up. He told me about the new family with the black cat, where he had hidden his rawhide chew, and . . .

"Zero-G, *please*." Funny how cranky you get when you're tired. And how you do things when you're half asleep. I reached over, the same way you do with a pesky alarm. Only with Zero-G, well, I think I might have touched the On-Off switch on his collar.

QUESTION 04:

Wait a minute. You "think" you "might" have shut off Zero-G's voice?

ANSWER 04:

Right. I think. I might have. I don't quite remember.

I must have made it back to my room, where I fell asleep. And I remember thinking as I drifted off . . .

He's just a dog.

New and
⑨ (Un)improved ✳ ✳ ✳

You would have thought I'd sleep and sleep and sleep after all that foo-fur-ah with Zero-G.

No such luck.

Instead, I rolled around on my bunk. Miko was trying to sleep on her floating anti-grav mat, and I probably kept her awake, too. (Miko and I share a room.)

Just a drone. Just a dog.

I tried sleeping on my back, and I tried counting comets. I prayed. (Not because it would put me to sleep, but because I needed to.) I even tried reading my Bible, but I had to stop after a while— after I ran into the part in Philippians about not letting pride be your guide. About being humble and looking out for others first.

The Adventures of DeeBee's Conscience, Episode 7

DeeBee's Conscience: *I am NOT letting you sleep. Not tonight.*

DeeBee: "Thanks a lot."

I had a problem, all right. And I figured I would be able to handle it better if I could only get some sleep.

Sleep, beautimous sleep. Was that all there was to fixing my problem?

$$* * *$$

The next morning, I shuffled out to get some breakfast. And no, I had not slept much at all.

Bee-ooop! My wrist interface flashed with a message from Buzz, then the same one from Miko.

"Hey, DeeBee," said the little talking 3-D head floating above my wrist. "How about breakfast with us today? You haven't eaten with us for the last couple of days."

I didn't even have to think about it. Perfect! I could tell them I was sorry over a plate full of duplicator eggs and pulsar cakes.

"Be right there," I promised as I stepped through my apartment door.

Did I say "right there"? It didn't quite work out that way. See, Percee Plasma had other ideas.

"Not so fast, young lady." Percee grabbed my arm as he hurried me down the hall, away from the dining hall. "We've got a lot of work to do this morning."

"But, breakfast—" I tried to explain.

"Ready for you on the set. Miss Neutron has ordered a gourmet catering drone. She's expecting you."

"Oh." I wrinkled my nose. I'd had enough of the gourmet catering drone's food by that time. *Gourmet* meant hoity-toity, fancy-shmantzy, full of weird mushroomy things and covered in rich sauces that make my stomach turn. I'd take good old leathery *CLEO*-cakes over shrimp soufflé any day.

But what could I do? I had to follow Percee to the stage. He went on and on about how to look into the camera better, how to use my voice best, the funniest kinds of jokes to try . . .

"Are you getting all this, Daphne?"

"Yessir."

Forty-five minutes later, I finally talked him into letting me take a few minutes for a potty break. I could have used my booster boots to blast down the halls, but I probably wouldn't have made it to the dining room any more quickly.

Swoosh! I almost burst down the dining room door.

"Well, well, if it isn't Miss Vid Star." Buzz was the first one to see me. He was carrying his empty tray to the door. But at least he was still there.

"Aren't you too busy to eat with us?" asked Miko. "We were going to call you again, but then we heard you were with Percee Plasma."

"Look, you guys." I had to explain. I had to tell them being famous wasn't as good as I'd thought it would be. And then I had to tell them I was sorry for being such a—

"Hey, DeeBee!" This time it was my brother, shuffling into the dining hall with Zero-G on his heels. "You should be proud of me."

"Proud?" I asked.

"Yeah. For fixing Zero-G's collar."

Uh-oh. Now the truth would come out.

"Weirdest thing." Tag bent down to show us the collar. "Somebody switched it off, or maybe he knocked it against something."

"That's correct." Zero-G looked straight at me. "Very odd, indeed."

That did it. I don't know if it was the look in Zero-G's eyes, not getting much sleep the night before, the Bible verses, or what.

But I had to settle this thing. Right here, right now.

"Look, everyone." I planted my feet and took a deep breath. The dining hall door swooshed open again behind me, but I didn't check to see who it was. "I'm really, really—"

"You are really, really late for the next show!" said Neta Neutron. "Where have you *been*? We have a schedule to keep."

Oh dear. How had she found me? I held my head with both hands and tried to pretend I was not in this mess. But Neta told me to follow her, and we had another show to shoot. I think she actually might have had a tow beam in her pocket.

At least, it felt like it.

"Can I talk to you guys later?" I yelled down the hall. "Let's do lunch."

"Yeah, sure," Tag answered. He looked out the dining hall door with the rest of the Astro-Kids.

"I liked the old mistress DeeBee Ortiz better," said Zero-G, just loudly enough for me to hear.

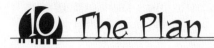 The Plan ✳ ✳ ✳

Want to know what scared me the most? I was actually starting to get used to doing the show—and being Daphne Orr, vid star and famous inventor.

"Show number three." Percee gave us the thumbs-up sign as the lights went out the next day. "That's a wrap. Great job."

Great? Sure, if you could believe Percee. He kept talking about a ninety-nine point nine rating, the best on any network in the solar system. Better than *Saturday Night Weightless Sumo Wrestling*. Better than *My Favorite Martian* reruns. Percee was sure worked up about it.

"This is even better than the *Venus Sisters*!" He chuckled and looked like he was washing his hands in the air.

Neta Neutron smiled, too. "I *knew* you would be big, dahling."

Big and phony. All I did was pull out bogus inventions and read the reader screen. The inventions weren't really mine, and neither were the words I said.

Even so, people ate it up. By the third day, I had 4,722,931 e-notes. I counted.

Can you believe it? Four million, seven hundred twenty-two thousand, nine hundred thirty-one. More every minute, too. Who was going to answer all that fan mail?

I had no idea. And you should have seen it when my face started popping up on wrist interface ads all over the solar system. You're minding your own business, and *bee-oop*, up pops my smiling face from your wrist interface.

"Today, at eleven, live from *CLEO-7*!" I couldn't believe it.

"That's my girl!" said my dad. He hardly ever said corny stuff like that. But he and my mom came to every show we did that week at the station.

Only now, things were starting to get really

serious. And I thought, *Do I really have a chance at being Neta Neutron's full-time co-host?*

I mean, from now on?

Anyone on the station would have said yes. Everyone told me, "This is your big chance."

But I had another question they couldn't answer: Did I want to take the job?

Neta Neutron would say, "Of course, dahling!" But she always said that.

My folks said we should pray about it. And we did. But I still wasn't sure what to do.

"I'm not doing it unless we can lose the phony inventions," I finally told Miko the night after the fourth show. And that's when we came up with (big background music, please) . . .

The Plan.

QUESTION 05:

What's "The Plan"? Sounds like a mystery.

ANSWER 05:

Stay tuned.

So there we were, on the set. The last day of

the show at *CLEO*-7. I winked at Miko. Everything would have to work perfectly, or Percee would figure it out.

"Everything ready for the last show?" Percee didn't miss a thing.

"All set," I answered, and then I winked at Miko. Nobody noticed when she slipped out the back row of seats.

And then the music came up and the room lights went down. People started clapping, the way they had been all week.

"Ladies and gentlemen . . ." Percee did his little wind-up with his hands. "It's Neeeeeta Neuuu-tron!"

(Clapping, clapping, et cetera.)

"And her special co-host, DAPH-neeeeeee ORR!"

I met Neta in the middle of the stage just as the smoke went *poof*. We both gave a little smile and a bow before we sat down in our two chairs.

So far, so good.

Neta's opening speech went pretty well, too. She's a pro, don't forget. She managed a couple of jokes, and then she got to the good part.

"And after a wonderful week here on *CLEO-7*, I'm happy to announce Miss Orr will be a finalist for the job of co-host of the *Neta Neutron Show*!"

That's when the station went wild. You should have seen my parents up in the audience. Everyone else was clapping and hooting, too.

But they hadn't seen my grand finale yet.

"So, Daphne, let's get straight to it." Neta leaned forward in her chair. She always did when it was time for my act. "Do you have some more of your amazing inventions for us today?"

The words on my reader drone started to come up.

But I didn't look at them. Instead, I smiled right into the drone-cam.

"I sure do. And I thought since this was my last show here at the station, I'd do something special. It's a surprise."

It sure was.

"Wonderful!" Neta looked happy, but I could see her grip the edge of her seat, where the drone-cam couldn't see. She didn't have to worry, though.

"Actually, I have an extra-special invention

today." I pointed to the background, where MAC was waiting. Yes, I'd powered him back up. He swooped down with the 3-second style helmet in his hands.

"Ah, ah . . ." Neta sounded as if she was going to sneeze.

"Don't worry. It's my 3-second style helmet. Here." I held it up. "All you do is key in what you want to look like, and in three seconds . . ."

I turned to the audience. "What look should we give our announcer, Percee Plasma?"

"Blond!" yelled a tekkie.

"Curly red!"

"Straight dark!"

Neta Neutron giggled and waved for Percee to come on stage. Everybody clapped and cheered. Percee, who was standing off to the side of the stage, pretended to be shy. But I think he really did not mind coming out to be famous for just a minute. He smiled at the audience.

He was still waving and smiling when I keyed in Blond and we lowered the helmet over his head.

RRRRRRR . . .

The 3-second style helmet sounded like a food duplicator. Maybe that's because I had used old food duplicator parts to build it. But never mind that. Three seconds later . . .

ZHREEEEEP!

Percee came out with a cool-looking blond cut. Perfectamundo.

"OOOOOhhhhh." The audience clapped, and Percee bowed.

"I can undo this, too," I told them. And in another three seconds, we had Percee right back to his old look.

"AAAAAhhhhh."

"My, you are full of surprises, aren't you?" By this time, Neta looked as if she was having fun, too. At least she wasn't gripping the sides of her chair anymore.

Neither was I. Because this was *my* invention, and these were *my* words.

Maybe Neta could be *my* co-host, and not the other way around.

But first things first. MAC held on to the style

helmet while I looked for my chance. I would try it one more time.

"Now, what look should we give Miss Neutron?" I asked the audience.

11 RRRRRRRR... ✳ ✳ ✳

Now the audience was going wild. You should have heard the clapping and cheering.

"I've always wanted to be a redhead," Neta Neutron told us. The drone-cams stayed on her. The whole solar system was watching. So, while MAC held it for her, she poked her head into the style helmet and wiggled her shoulders.

Everybody got really quiet.

"In three seconds!" I waved my hand and touched the control for carrot red.

RRRRRRR...

At first, I thought it was working great.

RRRRRRR...

Okay, so it had been a little more than three seconds.

RRRRRRR...

Uh-oh.

RRRRRRRR . . .

This was not good. I reached for the helmet . . .

ZHREEEEEP!

. . . and yanked it off before it barbequed Miss Neutron's hair.

"OOOOOhhhhh." The audience gasped for a second when they saw what was left of Neta Neutron's hair. Make that, fifteen billion people all over the solar system saw what was left.

I couldn't believe it, either.

THIS WAS NOT SUPPOSED TO HAPPEN!

"I don't understand. . . ." I really didn't.

And, oh so slowly, Neta Neutron reached up to touch her crop of what had once been wavy, shiny, beautiful, shoulder-length golden hair.

Only now it looked like a head full of skinny carrots.

I mean, *real* carrots. Not carrot red.

"Carrots are an excellent source of vitamin A," said MAC, who was still hanging around to watch.

The audience started giggling.

Neta shrieked, and the audience busted out

laughing. Maybe they thought it was part of the act.

"Wait!" I tried to tell her. "I can undo it."

Maybe I shouldn't have tried that. Although, I would say that the bright green grassy color was better than carrots.

Wouldn't you say so, too?

In my defense, I have to tell you I tried three times to get Neta Neutron back to normal. But her face only got redder and redder as her hair got greener and greener.

And then, she finally exploded.

"Enough!" she screamed. "I have never been so humiliated in my entire life!"

Humiliated, as in embarrassed, as in made fun of in front of billions of people. And that was not good. This was a blooper, all right. A super-duper blooper.

"I'm really sorry," I whispered. So much for a *Daphne Orr, Famous Inventor* show.

"You and that sorry excuse for a drone! I don't ever want to see you . . ." She threw down my poor 3-second style helmet as hard as she could. "AGAIN!"

The helmet broke into pieces, which was probably just as well. And even though I kept trying to tell Miss Neutron I was sorry, well, she wasn't listening anymore.

The show was over. Unplugged.

But you want to hear the weird part?

When I looked at the shattered 3-second style helmet on the floor, I actually felt pretty good. Maybe it wasn't so bad being a techno-nerd ... with friends. I felt like a heavy weight had lifted from my shoulders.

OKIQ. Okay, I Quit.

The Adventures of DeeBee's Conscience, Episode 8

DeeBee's Conscience: *Does that mean you're listening to me again?*

DeeBee: "I think so. But keep reading."

Anyway, that was how everything turned out. It hadn't exactly followed The Plan. But I'll bet you can guess what happened next.

Yep. Neta Neutron and Percee Plasma packed

up and went toodle-oo almost quicker than a 3-second style helmet can ruin a good day. They vowed never to come back to *CLEO*-7, dahling. And here's where we fast-forward the story twenty-four hours. . . .

✳ ✳ ✳

"I still don't understand it," I told the rest of the AstroKids in my shop the next day. We had collected the pieces of my 3-second style helmet and piled them on a table. "I had that thing working perfectly. The molecular optimizer was totally realigned, and—"

"There you go again." Tag called a time-out. "English. Tell us in English."

"Forget it. But I'm really sorry, guys."

"You don't have to say you're sorry again." Buzz held up his hand. "We're not mad at you anymore. And besides, you've already told us you're sorry about twenty times."

"Twenty-two point three," said MAC. He floated in the corner of the shop.

Point three? Oh well. I wanted to make sure

they knew I meant it. But there was something else I had to say, too.

"All right. But listen, everybody. I know the 3-second style helmet bit the dust, big time. But there's no way that thing could have gone wacko . . . unless somebody messed with it."

"*Messed* with it?" Miko asked.

I nodded.

Mir wrinkled his nose. "You're not saying it was one of *us*?"

I think we all knew what it came down to. Buzz would never have messed around with the helmet. He might be smart enough to do it, maybe, but he's way too nice. Miko would have died before she would even think of it. And Tag could hardly read the directions in the *Tekkie How-To Book*. That left . . .

"Hey, now, wait a minute." Mir held up his hands. "If you think . . . I . . . No way."

"Who else?" I asked.

"Hey, I did *not* wreck your 3-second thingie. Don't look at me. Why don't you ask MAC?"

"MAC?" I turned to my drone.

He was inspecting a pile of old circuits in the

corner, not looking at us.

No answer.

"Hello, MAC? Weren't you holding the helmet before Miss Neutron put it on?"

MAC started spinning and blinking the way he does when things are wrong. What in the world?

"I only meant to assist." MAC was spinning pretty good by then. I had to grab one of his hands to slow him down. "I did not want you to be a co-host. I did not want you to . . . want you to . . ."

What?

" . . . did not want you to leave."

"MAC monkeyed with the helmet?" Tag asked. "Cool!"

So that's what had happened. MAC was the one who reprogrammed the molecular optimizer . . . I mean, he messed up the 3-second style helmet.

4COL! As in, For Crying Out Loud!

"Please do not shut down my system," he begged. "On my honor, I promise I will never monkey with one of your inventions again. I am sorry."

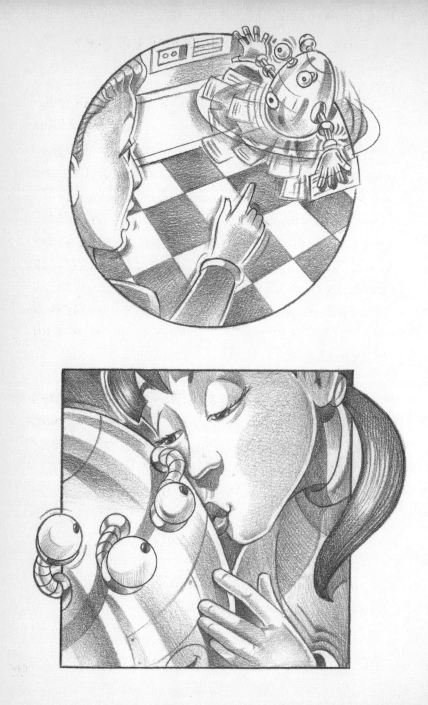

"You're sorry?" I asked. I thought about it for just a micro-minute. Then I reached over and planted a big kiss on MAC's warm metal side—about where his cheek would be. "I'm the one who's sorry."

"You are?"

"Yes." Funny how it took a big blowup to get my attention. Or to help me get my head on straight again. Or even to help me remember what the Bible said about putting other people first. I shivered at the thought. "You saved me from a lot of trouble."

"Well, of course I did, Mistress Daphne."

"AAGHH!" I threw up my hands, and it felt good to laugh with my friends again. Very good. "My name is DeeBee, okay? Don't anybody *ever* call me Daphne again!"

RealSpace Debrief

✳ ✳ ✳

Twinkle, Twinkle, Little Satellite

Remember when DeeBee and Tag were talking about how the *CLEO-7* station was in "geo-sink" orbit? That's short for *geosynchronous*. It describes the way a satellite orbits the Earth from a spot high above—and straight above—it. If that satellite spins around the Earth as fast as the Earth is turning, it looks as if it's standing still.

So what? That's what science fiction writer Arthur C. Clarke asked in a magazine article way back in 1945. Clarke's idea was to shoot up three satellites, park them in space, and use them to send TV signals around the world. Better than walkie-talkies, for sure.

Well, Clarke had the right idea. But no one

did anything about it until thirteen years later, in December of 1958. That's when the U.S. launched the world's first communications satellite, called SCORE. It was used to broadcast President Eisenhower's Christmas message, which quoted Luke 2:14: "On earth peace, good will toward men" KJV.

SCORE's batteries lasted only twelve days. Maybe the battery charger's cord didn't quite reach. But SCORE was only the start. By 1961, only three years later, the U.S. and the Soviet Union had already launched seventy-four satellites. Then other countries like the United Kingdom, Canada, and France followed. Some of the new satellites were in geosynchronous orbits, while others spun around the globe in different directions. Most got their power from solar chargers.

Today, satellites are very, very big business. Why? Because satellites are very handy for sending radio and TV signals all over the world—not to mention the Internet and secret military stuff. Weather satellites help us to see if it's going to snow, or if a hurricane is coming our way. You've seen those big pictures of clouds the weather people stand in front of? Most of those are taken from satellites, too.

But there's a lot more. From halfway across the world, we can watch a news reporter tell us about a war. Or we can see an Olympic swimmer break a world record—right when it happens. Computers talk to each other through satellites, too.

If you want to see a satellite for yourself, just look up at the sky on a dark night. You have a pretty good chance of sighting one, since there are over 8,600 known objects in Earth's orbit. ("Objects" are anything from lost astronaut tools to the International Space Station!)

The secret to spotting satellites is getting away from light. Glare from buildings and streetlights makes it really hard to see stars and satellites. That's partly because your eyes don't adjust as well when it's too bright.

But don't go satellite hunting alone. With your parents, get away from all the lights you can, like streetlights or porch lights. The darker, the better. The best time is forty-five minutes after sunset—or forty-five minutes before sunrise, if you're up that early—when the Earth's shadow isn't as much of a problem.

Be patient. If you are, sooner or later you'll notice something that looks like a bright star making its way across the sky. There's your satellite! It's bright because it reflects sunlight, just like the moon.

You should be able to see a satellite fine just by looking, but you might want to use a pair of binoculars or even a telescope for a better close-up view. Whatever you choose, don't forget that one of the first messages ever bounced off a satellite was from God's Word. And if you remember *that*, you can remember that it's our job to keep "bouncing" God's Word to the world, any way we can.

FTF (Face To Face), or even using satellites.

Want to find out more about satellites and what they do? Then check out a great Web site for kids, called The Space Place. The address is *http://space place.jpl.nasa.gov*. You can do space experiments, discover amazing space facts, and lots more. And for more on the history of satellites, check out (hold on to your hats!): *www.physics.udel.edu/~watson /scen103/projects/99s/satellites/firsts.html.*

And the Coded Message Is . . . ✳ ✳ ✳

You think this ASTROKIDS adventure is over? Not yet! Here's the plan: We'll give you the directions, you find the words. Write them all on a piece of paper. They form a secret message that has to do with *The Super-Duper Blooper*. If you think you got it right, log on to *www.elmerbooks.org* and follow the instructions there. You'll receive free ASTROKIDS wallpaper for your computer and a sneak peek at the next ASTROKIDS adventure. It's that simple!

WORD 1:
chapter 10, paragraph 5, word 9 _____

WORD 2:
chapter 9, paragraph 5, word 58 _____

WORD 3:
chapter 3, paragraph 28, word 8 _____

WORD 4:

chapter 1, paragraph 16, word 16 _____

WORD 5:

chapter 3, paragraph 8, word 5 _____

WORD 6:

chapter 11, paragraph 68, word 12 _____

WORD 7:

chapter 7, paragraph 21, word 7 _____

WORD 8:

chapter 9, paragraph 5, word 63 _____

WORD 9:

chapter 6, paragraph 3, word 15 _____

WORD 10:

chapter 2, paragraph 9, word 4 _____

WORD 11:

chapter 6, paragraph 17, word 8 _____

WRITE IT ALL HERE:

_____

_____

(Hint: DeeBee says to look up Philippians 2. Check your Bible!)

Contact Us! ✳ ✳ ✳

If you have any questions for the author or would just like to say hi, feel free to contact him at Bethany House Publishers, 11400 Hampshire Avenue South, Minneapolis, MN 55438, United States of America, EARTH. Please include a self-addressed, stamped envelope if you'd like a reply. Or log on to Robert's intergalactic Web site at *www.elmerbooks.org*. Robert also speaks and does writing workshops at schools and homeschool gatherings. For more info, just ask!

Launch
Countdown

* * *

AstroKids 08:
AstroBall Free-4-All

Zoing! Play astroball!

Astroball season is at hand, and Mir Chekhov's father has arranged for him to be *CLEO-7*'s team captain. Problem is, Mir hasn't ever played the game before, and it's tough to learn on the fly—especially with the All-*CLEO* AstroBall Tournament just around the corner. If only the AstroKids didn't have to play Deeter Meteor and the other kids from *CLEO-5*!

Yes, Deeter is back, and Mir wants to stop him in his high and mighty tracks. At the same time, Mir wants to prove himself to his dad. Actually, just getting his busy father's attention would be a good start.

That's when Mir finds out about Nep2nade C and the incredible ChampVision. Will Mir and the AstroKids do *anything* to win?

Series for Young Readers*
From Bethany House Publishers

THE ADVENTURES OF CALLIE ANN
by Shannon Mason Leppard
Readers will giggle their way through the true-to-life escapades of Callie Ann Davies and her many North Carolina friends.

ASTROKIDS™
by Robert Elmer
Space scooters? Floating robots? Jupiter ice cream? Blast into the future for out-of-this-world, zero-gravity fun with the AstroKids on space station *CLEO-7.*

BACKPACK MYSTERIES
by Mary Carpenter Reid
This excitement-filled mystery series follows the mishaps and adventures of Steff and Paulie Larson as they strive to help often-eccentric relatives crack their toughest cases.

THE CUL-DE-SAC KIDS
by Beverly Lewis
Each story in this lighthearted series features the hilarious antics and predicaments of nine endearing boys and girls who live on Blossom Hill Lane.

JANETTE OKE'S ANIMAL FRIENDS
by Janette Oke
Endearing creatures from the farm, forest, and zoo discover their place in God's world through various struggles, mishaps, and adventures.

THREE COUSINS DETECTIVE CLUB®
by Elspeth Campbell Murphy
Famous detective cousins Timothy, Titus, and Sarah-Jane learn compelling Scripture-based truths while finding—and solving—intriguing mysteries.

*(ages 7–10)

Series for Middle Graders* From BHP

ADVENTURES DOWN UNDER • by Robert Elmer
When Patrick McWaid's father is unjustly sent to Australia as a prisoner in 1867, the rest of the family follows, uncovering action-packed mystery along the way.

ADVENTURES OF THE NORTHWOODS • by Lois Walfrid Johnson
Kate O'Connell and her stepbrother Anders encounter mystery and adventure in northwest Wisconsin near the turn of the century.

BLOODHOUNDS, INC. • by Bill Myers
Hilarious, hair-raising suspense follows brother-and-sister detectives Sean and Melissa Hunter in these madcap mysteries with a message.

GIRLS ONLY! • by Beverly Lewis
Four talented young athletes become fast friends as together they pursue their Olympic dreams.

MANDIE BOOKS • by Lois Gladys Leppard
With over five million sold, the turn-of-the-century adventures of Mandie and her many friends will keep readers eager for more.

PROMISE OF ZION • by Robert Elmer
Following WWII, thirteen-year-old Dov Zalinsky leaves for Palestine—the one place he may still find his parents—and meets the adventurous Emily Parkinson. Together they experience the dangers of life in the Holy Land.

THE RIVERBOAT ADVENTURES • by Lois Walfrid Johnson
Libby Norstad and her friend Caleb face the challenges and risks of working with the Underground Railroad during the mid–1800s.

TRAILBLAZER BOOKS • by Dave and Neta Jackson
Follow the exciting lives of real-life Christian heroes through the eyes of child characters as they share their faith with others around the world.

THE YOUNG UNDERGROUND • by Robert Elmer
Peter and Elise Andersen's plots to protect their friends and themselves from Nazi soldiers in World War II Denmark guarantee fast-paced action and suspenseful reads.

*(ages 8–13)

Great Stories for New Readers!

Fun, humorous, and written just for beginning readers, YOUNG COUSINS MYSTERIES™, a prequel series to THREE COUSINS DETECTIVE CLUB®, are early-reader first chapter mysteries. With full-color illustrations and written in a style just for new readers, these are a valuable addition to any child's bookshelf.

BY ELSPETH CAMPBELL MURPHY

The Birthday Present Mystery
The Sneaky Thief Mystery
The Giant Chicken Mystery
The Chalk Drawings Mystery

www.elspethcampbellmurphy.com

BETHANY BACKYARD®

11400 Hampshire Ave. S., Minneapolis, MN 55438
1-800-328-6109 www.bethanyhouse.com